Missouri

Double Trouble Series

Daina Sargent has lived in several states but considers Arkansas her home. Born in California and raised in Arkansas, she graduated from West Fork High School with honors in 1981. Daina attended college in Jonesboro, Arkansas and Tulsa, Oklahoma. She plans to continue her education. Daina has three daughters.

Missouri

Double Trouble Series

By Daina Sargent

Illustrated by Jane Lenoir

Ozark Publishing, Inc.
P.O. Box 228
Prairie Grove, AR 72753

Cataloging-in-Publication Data

Sargent, Daina, 1963–
    Missouri / by Daina Sargent ; illustrated by
Jane Lenoir. —Prairie Grove, AR : Ozark
Publishing, c2005.
        p. cm. (Double trouble series)

    "Teamwork"—Cover.
    SUMMARY: Matt and Liz travel through
time to Hannibal, Missouri and have the
opportunity to ride a raft down the mighty
Mississippi River with Tom Sawyer and
Huck Finn. When they get into trouble,
they have to work together with Huck and
Tom to get to safety.
        ISBN 1-59381-126-8 (hc)
              1-59381-127-6 (pbk)
        1. Missouri—Juvenile fiction.
2. Rafting—Juvenile fiction. 3. River—
Juvenile fiction. [1. Missouri—Fiction.
2. Rafting—Fiction. 3. River—Fiction]
I. Sargent, Daina, 1963– II. Jane Lenoir, 1950– ill.
III. Title. IV. Series.
        PZ7.S24Mi 2005
        [Fic]—dc21   2003099974

Copyright © 2005 by Daina Sargent
All rights reserved

Printed in the United States of America

iv

Inspired by

When looking at my daddy, you think that he's just an ordinary man. However when you get to know him, you will see that he is an incredibly intelligent man, worth a diamond in the heart. He is better compared to a diamond in the rough.

Dedicated to

I would like to dedicate this to the 2003 conference-winning Prairie Grove Tigers, especially the seniors! Great job, Team!

Foreword

Matt and Liz travel through time to Hannibal, Missouri and have the opportunity to ride a raft down the mighty Mississippi River with Tom Sawyer and Huck Finn. When they get into trouble, they have to work together with Huck and Tom to get to safety.

Contents

One	Tom and Huck	1
Two	The Raft	11
Three	The Slick Red Clay	23
Four	Missouri Facts	29

Missouri

Double Trouble Series

If you would like to have the author of the Double Trouble Series visit your school, free of charge, call 1-800-321-5671.

One

Tom and Huck

The Mississippi River is a mighty river that many people have floated down. Two people who traveled the mighty Mississippi were Huckleberry Finn and Tom Sawyer. Huck and Tom were the best of friends. The two young men were very mischievous and superstitious.

Huck Finn was a tall lanky, red-headed scallywag who looked a lot like Matt. Huck didn't pay attention to the rules, so he was feared by adults for such careless behavior.

1

However, he seemed to be a very practical young man.

Tom Sawyer, on the other hand, was a bit more fanciful. He was the leader in their adventures because he had the more active imagination.

Huck always went along with the adventures for the fun of it. He was never known to sit back and watch.

There were other differences between Tom and Huck. Huck had a lazy lifestyle and all kinds of freedom. He did not have a role model, and this allowed him to roam the streets. Tom, on the other hand, lived with his Aunt Polly and was well disciplined.

The twins had decided to read a book written by author Mark Twain. The book was about Tom Sawyer and Huckleberry Finn. They wanted their next adventure to take them to the state of Missouri.

Matt was sitting on the floor, leaning back against the wall, facing the oval, floor-length magic mirror.

He had already pulled the book from the shelf and had it in his hand when Liz walked in. He grinned at her and raised his eyebrows

Liz glanced at the mirror, took a deep breath, and began reading from the book Matt handed her.

She had read for maybe fifteen minutes when suddenly the big oval mirror began lighting up. Rainbows of light flashed around the room, and the twins looked at each other and smiled. They knew their adventure was beginning.

Matt sat back on his beanbag and pushed his glasses up on his nose, ready for their next adventure. He was a bit more excited about this adventure because they were going to be with the kings of adventure, Huckleberry Finn and Tom Sawyer.

Matt and Liz went through their mirror.

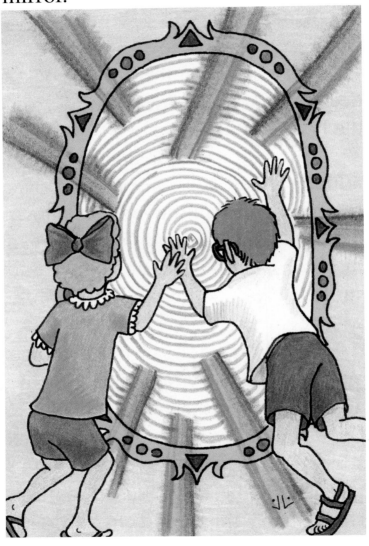

The twins found themselves in the year 1876, floating on a raft down the Mississippi River.

Matt and Liz were dressed in tattered clothing that consisted of overalls and cotton shirts. They were barefooted. And, as Matt had suspected, none other than the famous Huck Finn and Tom Sawyer were on the raft with them.

The two boys were surprised by the magical appearance of the twins. Huck had to take a second look to make sure he wasn't looking in a mirror when he saw Matt. Huck and Matt looked a lot alike. Tom was taken by the cute little Elizabeth.

"Who are you and what are you doin' here?" asked Huck.

"Well, I am Elizabeth Natasha. You may call me Liz. And this is my brother, Matt." After Liz had made the introductions, she asked, "Where are we?"

"Well, Miss Liz," replied Huck with a sarcastic note to his voice. "You are on the Mississippi River at Hannibal, Missouri. Now you can't be no dead weight on this-here raft, so grab yourself a stick and get to work getting us down this-here river."

Liz was not one who liked to be shown up by a boy, and her temper started rising. She was becoming very irritated with this young man. "What do you mean, grab a stick? I only see two, and you boys have both of them! If you want help, quit flapping your jaws and give me one!"

The sticks were long poles they used to push the raft in the water.

Huck handed his pole over to Liz. He didn't do much talking to her after that. He could tell she was a feisty one, and didn't want to rub her the wrong way. They were going to be on that raft for a while.

Two

The Raft

Tom and Matt were getting acquainted. They had hit it off better than Liz and Huck had.

"So, where you boys headed?" asked Matt.

"We ain't headin' anywhere in particular, Matt," Tom answered. "We're just goin'."

Matt told the boys about the adventures he and Liz had been on.

Tom listened closely to the tales Matt told. Tom was becoming quite envious of the twins. He loved adventures, and to have that mirror they had at home had to be fun.

After they traveled down the river for a couple of hours, the water became a little choppy. The small raft started rocking from side-to-side. With nothing to hang on to, the children stood in the middle of the raft, hoping they would be able to stay afloat. The sky darkened. Flickers of lightning now cast a lot of light. The claps of thunder were almost unbearable. Huck tried to stay calm and collected. Not much bothered him. Tom was a bit scared. And Matt and Liz were terrified!

"Oh my gosh! What do we do now?" Matt yelled at Tom.

"Just hang on to that sister of yours. She's so little she could blow away in the wind. Huck and me will try to fix things up and get us to the shore where we can be safe," Tom said, trying to reassure Matt.

Liz watched in amazement as Huck and Tom worked in unison. They knew how to work the poles to move the raft down the river.

Liz was holding Matt's hand tight, when THUD! There was a loud crash. She had shut her eyes tightly and was holding back tears of fear. When the crash happened, she held Matt's hand even tighter. Poor Matt thought that even though she was a tiny girl, she sure could squeeze tight. "What's happening, Matt," she asked.

"I don't know yet, Liz," he replied. He was still watching the two boys.

Tom and Huck had managed to get the raft to the bank of the river. They were trying to get off and tie the raft to a tree. The winds were blowing fiercely and the rain was pouring. Lightning and thunder were still crashing in the sky, and Liz could see fear in the boys' eyes.

"Hey, you two," Tom yelled. "We got us a cave 'round here that nobody knows 'bout. We's goin' there and wait out this-here storm."

Huck added, "You can come along, or sit here like a bump on a log. We ain't waitin' on you."

So off into the woods the four youngsters went. Matt and Liz were barefooted. They weren't used to being barefoot, walking through the terrain that they were heading through now. Liz was getting stickers in her toes. Matt had already stepped on something slimy. He didn't bother to look down to see what it was. He just knew he didn't like the way it felt on his feet.

When they got to the cave, the twins found out that Tom and Huck were quite the tour guides. They were also very smart about stocking supplies. They had matches and dry wood, and they managed to start a campfire.

Tom and Huck also had a little food with them.

Even though Huck had been a bit sarcastic toward Liz earlier, he tried easing some of the hostility now by offering her something to eat. "Want some soda crackers, Liz?" he asked.

She was a little surprised by his gesture. She took one from his hand with a sheepish, "Thanks, Huck."

Tom and Huck had also stored blankets in their cave.

"Do you two stay out often?" Matt asked. "How do you do it? Doesn't anyone miss you when you don't come home at night? Liz and I would be in so much trouble!"

"Oh shoot! My pa don't even know when I ain't home," said Huck.

Tom added, "We don't do it much, but when we do, we just do! Ain't no one knows where we are, so nobody knows where to look for us. I sure do get me a whopping from my Aunt Polly when I do go home. But it's worth it. 'Cause I sure do like comin' out here!"

The foursome sat and chatted a little while longer about different adventures. They were very sleepy from fighting the storm. They all drifted to sleep and took a short nap. The blankets that were handed out earlier, along with the fire, made the small cave cozy and warm.

When everyone awoke, Tom and Huck decided to walk toward the river. They wanted to catch a few fish to put on the fire to cook and eat. Everyone was quite hungry.

Little did Matt and Liz know, but the cave was also supplied with all kinds of fishing equipment.

Huck and Tom grabbed cane poles that had little strings tied to the ends of them. Tied on each string was a hook and a small rock that was used for a weight. Each of the boys had two poles, one in each hand.

"Get off your behinds and come on a walkin' with us. We've got to get some grub to eat," hollered Huck. "We don't catch and share unless you are out there tryin' to catch your own fish. You have to do your own work!"

"What on earth is he talking about, Matt?" asked Liz.

"I think he wants us to go with them and catch our own fish for our dinner!" Matt answered.

The four youngsters headed out
for the fishing hole with their poles.

Matt was excited. Here he was with Huck Finn and Tom Sawyer. He had read stories about their adventures, and here he was with them in person.

Three

The Slick Red Clay

As the four were walking to the river, they stopped on the bank to check on the raft. Tom and Huck wanted to look for any damage it might have.

Matt and Liz were not used to walking in red clay. They hit the clay at a pretty good clip. When Matt began sliding, he automatically reached out and grabbed Liz. They lost their balance and slid down the bank. They yelled for help, but Tom and Huck were ahead of them.

After gaining their composure, the twins held hands more tightly and tried to walk with Tom and Huck.

Just as she was about to cast her pole with the bait into the water, Liz slipped. Matt grabbed hold of her hand and held tight, but they kept sliding. He couldn't stop them from falling into the river.

Tom and Huck heard all the commotion. They dropped their poles and ran over to see what the twins were yelling about.

They looked all up and down the river bank. But they didn't see Matt and Liz

"Where do you reckon they are, Tom?" Huck said.

Just then, they saw Matt's clay-covered feet go beneath the water.

When Matt and Liz landed on their beanbags back in the library, they were dry. They had shoes on their feet and were neatly dressed.

"WOW, that was fun, wasn't it Liz?" Matt asked with so much delight.

"No, it was not!" Liz said. That Huckleberry Finn was not very nice! Although, when we needed help, like in the cave, he gave it to us. I thought Tom Sawyer was okay, for a boy."

Liz lay back on her beanbag and said, "Matt, I'm tired today. Can we wait a day or two before we read another story?"

"Sure we can, Liz," Matt said with a nod. Besides, it looks like it might rain in the next day or so. I want to go to the river and look around at something," said Matt.

"Count me out, Matt. You can go alone!" Liz was through with river adventures. At least for now!

Four

Missouri Facts

Map of Missouri

State Flag

State Bird: Bluebird

State Flower: Hawthorn

State Tree: Flowering Dogwood

Agriculture: Cattle, soybeans, hogs, dairy products, corn, poultry and eggs

Did you know that the most destructive tornado on record occurred in Annapolis, Missouri? It tore through the town on March 18, 1925, leaving a 980-foot-wide trail of demolished buildings, uprooted trees, and overturned cars.

Something unique: Missouri's state animal is the mule.